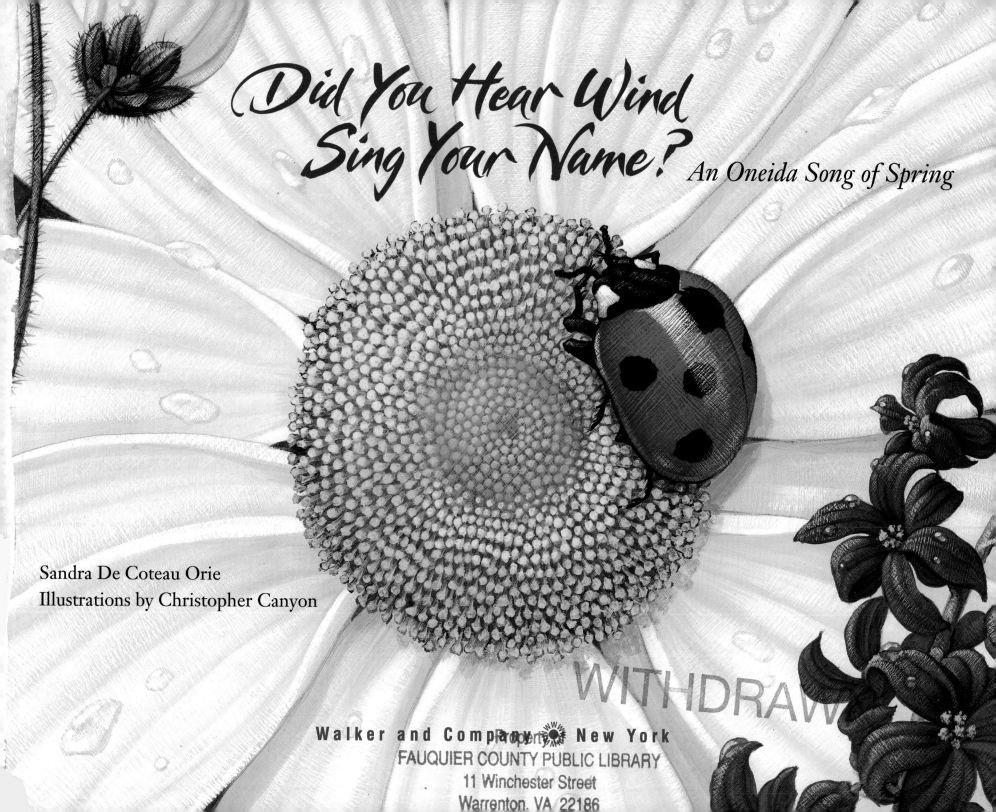

# Did You Hear Wind Sing Your Name?

## An Oneida Song of Spring

Sandra De Coteau Orie
Illustrations by Christopher Canyon

Walker and Company · New York

Elements of nature are personified in the Oneida culture to reflect the people's deep relationship with the natural world; capitalization in the text reflects this tradition.

The illustrations on these opening pages are the artist's representation of Oneida beadwork, which is the traditional form of artistic expression for the Oneida people.

First published in the United States of America in 1995 by Walker Publishing Company, Inc.

Published simultaneously in Canada by Thomas Allen & Son Canada, Limited, Markham, Ontario

Library of Congress Cataloging-in-Publication Data

De Coteau Orie, Sandra.

    Did you hear Wind sing your name? : an Oneida song of spring / Sandra De Coteau Orie ; illustrations by Christopher Canyon.

      p.  cm.

    Summary: Pictures and words pay homage to the Oneida Indians' view of the cycle of spring.

    ISBN 0-8027-8350-3. —ISBN 0-8027-8351-1 (reinforced)

    [1. Spring—Fiction.  2. Nature—Fiction.  3. Oneida Indians—Fiction. 4. Indians of North America—Fiction.]  I. Canyon, Christopher, ill.  II. Title.

PZ7.D3585Di  1995

[E]—dc20
                            94-31102

                                CIP

                                AC

Printed in Hong Kong

10  9  8  7  6  5  4  3  2  1

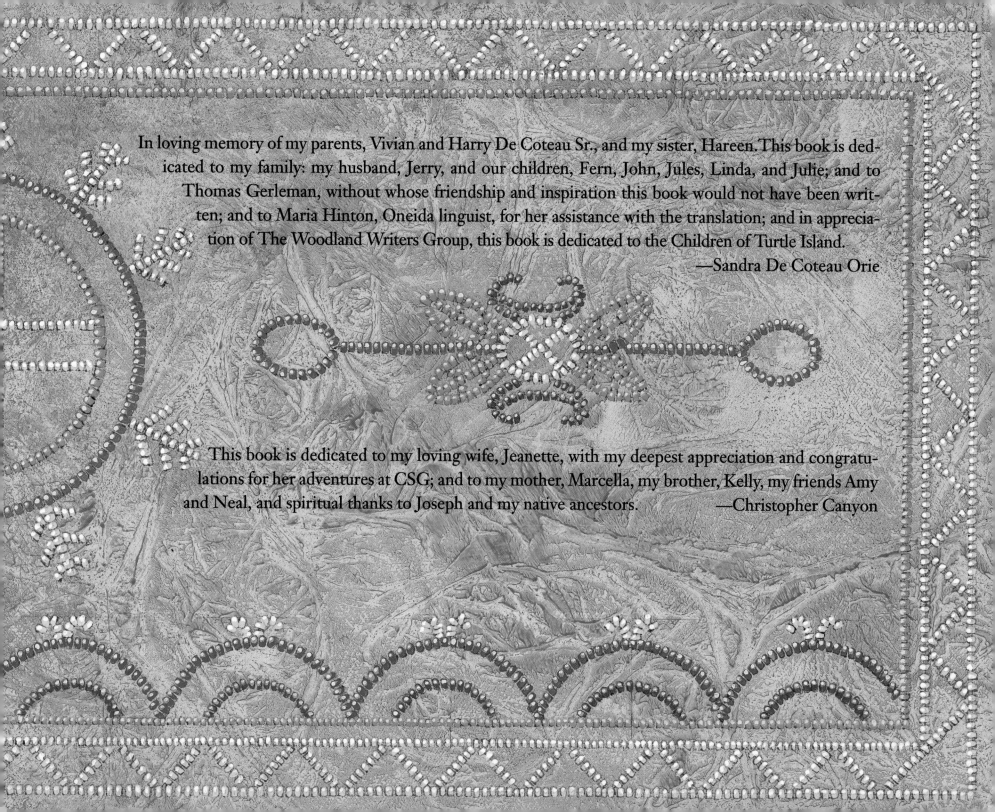

In loving memory of my parents, Vivian and Harry De Coteau Sr., and my sister, Hareen. This book is dedicated to my family: my husband, Jerry, and our children, Fern, John, Jules, Linda, and Julie; and to Thomas Gerleman, without whose friendship and inspiration this book would not have been written; and to Maria Hinton, Oneida linguist, for her assistance with the translation; and in appreciation of The Woodland Writers Group, this book is dedicated to the Children of Turtle Island.

—Sandra De Coteau Orie

This book is dedicated to my loving wife, Jeanette, with my deepest appreciation and congratulations for her adventures at CSG; and to my mother, Marcella, my brother, Kelly, my friends Amy and Neal, and spiritual thanks to Joseph and my native ancestors.

—Christopher Canyon

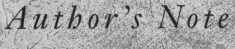

## Author's Note

*"Did you feel the great white roots of Pine beneath your feet centering you to Mother Earth?"*

The Pine tree historically symbolizes the unity of the Six Nations of the Iroquois Confederacy. The Pine's great white roots extend to the Six Nations: the Oneida, Mohawk, Seneca, Cayuga, Onondaga, and Tuscarora, who are named the Haudenosaunee, or The People of the Longhouse.

Other Oneida worldviews include the importance of the Hawk, the bringer of good news; our sustaining Elder Brother Sun; and the recognition of Cedar and Sweet Grass used in our ceremonies.

The Three Sisters—Corn, Beans, and Squash—are very important to Oneida people, for they are our sustaining staples and have helped the ONʌYOTÉÁ•KA, or Oneida, called "The People of the Standing Stone," to survive. Historically these foods have been planted together in the same fields; the Bean vines wrap themselves around the Cornstalks, and the Squash plants provide ground cover.

The flowers give us beauty, and, like the first flowers of the woodlands—the Trilliums—they announce Spring's arrival. The Strawberries, being the first fruits of the season, are celebrated, as are all forms of life in the continuing sacred circle.

This book is a celebration of the circle of life—the return of morning to night as well as of each cycle of the seasons.

It is a song, and in the Oneida language, to sing means to give thanks. You are invited in this thanksgiving.

*Traveling North*
*Did you see*
*Spirit Hawk dancing on the Wind?*

*Did you feel
morning Sun's warmth upon your face
welcoming you to a new day?*

*Did you see
the White Birch standing tall among the Darkwoods
and the greening of the Aspen Saplings?*

*Did you smell
the sweet scent of the sacred Cedar?*

*D*id you see
the fields of the Three Sisters
coming?

Did you see
Sun's face in the Buttercup?
And did you see Sky's blue in the wildwood Violets?

$D$id you greet
the Four-leggeds
and celebrate the Winged-One's
dances?

*Did you trace
Turtle's tracks along the Creek
and know you weren't alone?*

*Did you hear*
*Wind sing your name?*
*Does your memory bring Sweet Grass's fragrance?*

*Did you taste
the Thunderer's moist sky Waters?
Were you healed by Meadow's wild
Strawberries?*

Did your eyes catch Sunset's burgundy?
Did you see Trillium's Stars
lying upon the Forest bed's heaven?

Did you sense
Grandmother Moon guiding you
home again?

Did your heart
bring home the songs of all These living?